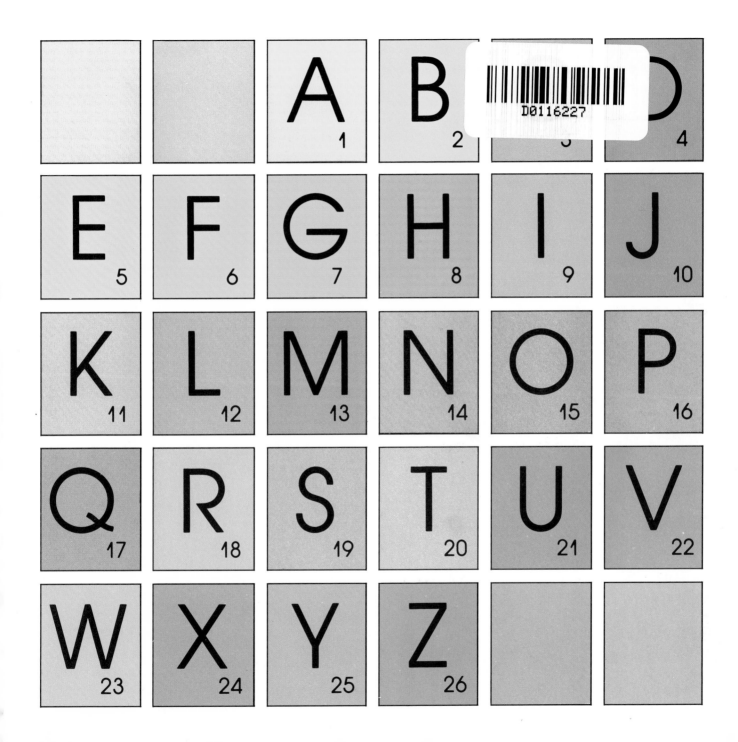

Humbug Potion

an A • B • Cipher

by Lorna Balian

ABINGDON PRESS

NASHVILLE

for Anoush Anne with love

HUMBUG POTION
Copyright © 1984 by Lorna Balian

Library of Congress Cataloging in Publication Data

Balian, Lorna.
  Humbug potion.
  Summary: A homely witch is delighted to find a secret recipe for beauty but it is written in a code that the reader must help her decipher by learning the letters of the alphabet.
  [1. Witches—Fiction. 2. Alphabet. 3. Literary recreations] I. Title.
PZ7.B1978Hp 1984   [E]   83-15808

ISBN 0-687-18021-X

Manufactured in the United States of America

There was this witch...

and all of her was homely.
You can see for yourself—
head to toe, she really was homely!

She longed to be beautiful.
It was her dearest wish.

Imagine her delight when she discovered an old recipe for a Magic Beauty Potion. The recipe was written in a secret code, but she was eager to become beautiful and determined to decipher it.

Aa

1

"Into a large cauldron drop an   1-3-15-18-14.

Bb

2

Add a   2-9-20   of a witch's   2-18-15-15-13

Cc

3

and a   3-21-16   of   3-15-4   liver oil.

Dd

4

Sift   4-18-25   4-9-18-2O   around   the   rim

Ee

5

and break in eight rotten 5-7-7-19.

Ff

6

Add five   6-9-19-8

Gg
7

and a bunch of   7-18-5-5-14   7-18-1-16-5-19.

Hh

8

Slip in a 8-1-9-18 from the head of a 8-5-14,

along with an 9-14-19-5-3-2O or two.

Jj

10

Add a 10-1-18 of 10-5-12-12-25

Kk

and an old house   11-5-25.

LI

12

Cut in a little 12-1-3-5 from a petticoat.

Mm

13

Flavor with the squeak of a   13-15-21-19-5.

Nn

A rusty 14-1-9-12 would be nice,

along with one sliced   15-14-9-15-14.

Pp
16

Then add a   16-1-9-12   of   16-5-1-19

Qq

17

and a   17-21-9-12-12   from a   17-21-1-9-12.

Rr
18

Slide in a   18-5-4   18-9-2-2-15-14,

Ss
19

some   19-15-1-16,   and a   smelly   19-8-15-5.

Toss in 20-23-15   20-5-5-20-8.

Uu

21

Stir with an   21-13-2-18-5-12-12-1   and a   19-13-9-12-5."

(She was so impatient to become beautiful, she ignored the 19-13-9-12-5.)

Vv

22

"Add a bunch of   22-9-15-12-5-20-19,

Ww

23

with lots of slimy   23-1-20-5-18,
and some   23-15-15-12   from a   23-15-12-6.

Now put in some 11-9-19-19-5-19 from a letter,

Yy

25

a yellow   25-15 – 25-15,

and the petals from a purple 26-9-14-14-9-1.

Stir carefully—
strain through a torn stocking—and DRINK EVERY DROP."

Hmmmmm.   It didn't work.

No!   It really did not work! Tsk! Tsk!
Perhaps the 19-13-9-12-5 would have helped.

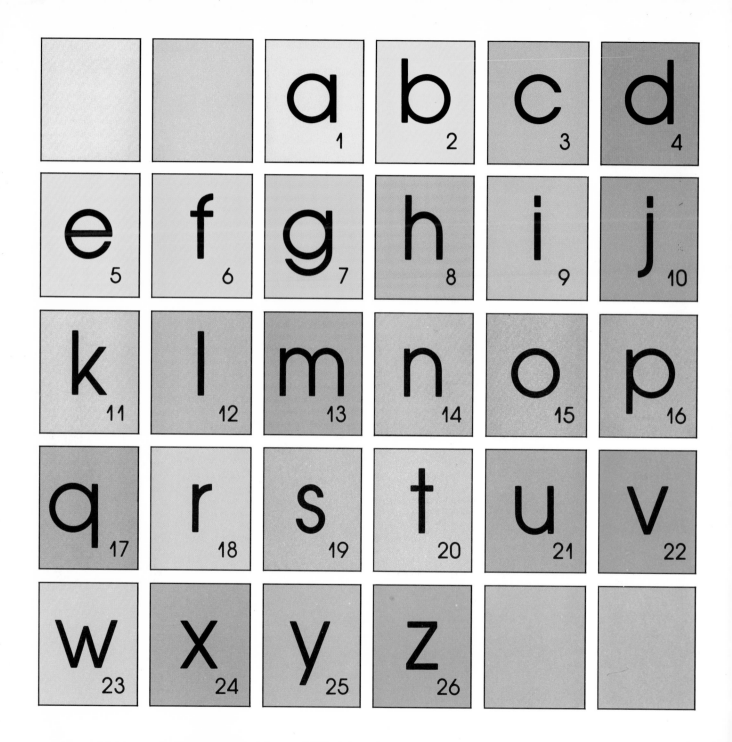